For my niece, Megan Flaherty – E. F.

For Marc, Laura and Megan – O. W.

The Mermaid of Cafur

Written by EVELYN FOSTER
Illustrated by OLWYN WHELAN

BAREFOOT BOOKS

Far away to the west, there is a magical underwater kingdom called Cafur, deep beneath the dark, emerald sea. If you look carefully on days when the wind is still, you can sometimes see the rooftops of the town: tall steeples and bent gables and the crowns of ancient trees. And if you visit the seashore at night, you can see lights that glow like tiny jewels, and hear bells that ring out like silver.

At the heart of the kingdom of Cafur stands a castle. It has turrets of pearl and sapphire, and its towers are guarded by huge seahorses with glittering manes. If you are lucky, you may also catch a glimpse of the sea folk. With their webbed bodies and their long green hair, they are strange, unearthly and beautiful.

ong ago, the kingdom of Cafur had a
magnificent queen called Arianne. People
said that she was lovelier by far than any
mortal woman, and it was true. Arianne was
a beautiful mermaid, with skin as white as a
gull's wing and a voice like the song of the
harp. But her eyes were as hard as stones and
her heart was cruel. For miles around, people
feared her, because Arianne stole children
and dragged them beneath the waves to serve
her. When she tired of them, she turned them
into sea bass.

One summer evening, Arianne swam to the surface of the sea and saw a mortal boy called Ewan. As soon as she saw him, she wanted him for her own.

Now Ewan was a farm boy who loved to walk on the shore beside the sea when his work was finished. Every evening he walked barefoot on the warm, white sand, and every day Arianne watched him. She swam close to the shore and talked to Ewan, tempting him with tales of her kingdom. She promised him gold, she promised him jewels, she promised to make him immortal, if only he would leave the land and live with her beneath the waves.

But Ewan loved the land; he loved his dog, Merlin; and most of all, he loved his sister, Meaghan. So he refused the offers of the beautiful mermaid, and he was silent when she mocked him.

Each time Ewan refused to go with Arianne, she wanted him even more. So she bided her time beneath the cold green waves. At last, she came up with a cruel plan. The next time she saw Ewan on the beach, she sang to him of the beauty of the sunrise. "The sea may look beautiful in the evening," she told him, "but unless you have seen it, you cannot imagine how lovely it is at dawn. Come and see, come and see!"

For Ewan did not know, but Arianne knew, that there was a spell on Cafur. Every year on the first of May, at sunrise, the town rose up above the water; any mortal who saw it would be drawn by enchantment into its streets. And when the sun was fully risen, the town disappeared, trapping them there forever.

Ewan suspected nothing. Wanting to see the beauty of the sea at dawn, he woke up early the next day, which was May morning, and set out. He was astonished at the sight of the magical town, and ventured in at its gate. Arianne was ready. With a cry of greedy joy, she seized him, and dragged him beneath the waves.

In her castle, the mermaid gave Ewan a strange, ruby wine. It tasted so sweet that Ewan drank it all. But as soon as he had swallowed it, he forgot the land. He forgot his home, he forgot his dog, and he even forgot his sister, Meaghan.

But Meaghan did not forget him. Meaghan was brave, loyal and true. When Ewan did not return, she cried for seven days and seven nights, and even Merlin could not comfort her. At last, Meaghan dried her tears. She knew that if she wanted to rescue Ewan, she would need the help of the sea witch.

Now the sea witch lived in a cave at the edge of the western sea. The door of the cave was guarded by three sea dogs, the cousins of dogs who live on land. Few people had met the sea dogs and lived to tell the tale.

But Meaghan was not thinking of the sea dogs. She thought only of her brother, Ewan. Taking Merlin with her, she walked and she walked until she came at last to the entrance of the cave. When she saw the sea dogs, she did not fear them. And because she had a land dog with her, and was not afraid, the sea dogs let her pass.

*M*eaghan and Merlin walked a long, long way down a wet, dark tunnel and into a chamber of silver. The room blazed and sparkled with the light from silver treasures of every kind — finely wrought cups and dishes; huge bowls and trophies and boxes of exquisite earrings, bracelets and necklaces. With her hand on Merlin's collar, Meaghan walked straight through the chamber of silver. Next, they came to a chamber of gold. Here the treasures were even brighter than in the chamber of silver. Again, Meaghan walked straight through. And because she did not touch any of the treasure, she was allowed to pass in safety. Had she so much as touched one silver teaspoon, she would have been turned at once to cold stone.

*A*t last, Meaghan and Merlin reached a winding staircase that led to the witch's tower. Up and up and up turned the staircase, and Meaghan and Merlin turned with it. As they rounded the last bend, they came face to face with a dragon, and what a dragon it was! As soon as it saw them, it opened its huge jaws and belched orange fire and roared until the whole staircase shook. But Meaghan stood still and did not flinch, and the dragon crumbled to dust.

*T*he door of the tower flew open and there sat the sea witch. She had hair as tangled as seaweed and eyes as old as the moon. Slowly, with Merlin beside her, Meaghan went up to the sea witch. The witch beckoned to her. "Come in, child," she said, "for by your courage so far, I have already decided to help you. Come, and tell me your trouble."

Then Meaghan told the sea witch of her brother Ewan and how he had disappeared. The sea witch closed her eyes and saw Ewan in the power of the mermaid. Then she looked deep into Meaghan's eyes and asked what she would do to save Ewan.

"He is my brother," Meaghan told her. "I will do anything to save him."

"Would you even give up your most cherished possession?" asked the sea witch.

"To help my brother," said Meaghan, "I would give up life itself."

"I do not want your life," replied the sea witch. "But in return for my help, you must leave your dog here." The sea witch leaned forward and laid her hand on Merlin's collar.

Then Meaghan shook from the soles of her feet to the roots of her hair and her face turned pale. But Merlin walked quietly to the witch and lay at her feet. Though her heart ached, Meaghan knew that he would be safe with the sea witch, so she did not try to stop him. Now the witch knew that Meaghan did indeed love her brother. For a love as true and strong as this, she was prepared to share her wisdom.

"Listen carefully," the sea witch told Meaghan. "There is one thing that Arianne cannot withstand, and that is the touch of iron. For iron is of the earth itself, and has the powers of the earth behind it. If you fight the mermaid with iron, you have a chance. But Arianne is dangerous, and once in her realm, you are in peril."

Then the sea witch gave Meaghan an old, iron-bladed knife. "To enter the kingdom of Cafur," she said, "you will have to wait another year until the first day of May. Guard this knife safely and be sure to take it with you." Then she wished Meaghan well and ordered her monsters to let the girl pass.

M eaghan kept the iron-bladed knife with her every day, and every night she slept with it under her pillow. And so a year passed. Then, on the first of May, Meaghan woke early and walked to the shore before sunrise. The kingdom of Cafur rose up onto the land, and Meaghan stepped boldly into it. She made her way straight through the town to the mermaid's castle of pearl and sapphire. The walls were hung with tapestries and the floors were white with shells. As Meaghan walked, sea bass brushed against her skirts, but everything around her was silent.

In the center of the castle, Meaghan saw Ewan. He was sitting on a lonely throne, drinking wine from a heavy goblet. "Ewan!" Meaghan shouted, and she ran to him. But Ewan looked straight through her. Meaghan was nearly in despair. Then she remembered the knife. She touched him with its blade, and at once her brother's eyes were opened and he embraced her.

Then Meaghan touched one of the sea bass with the blade of the knife, and it turned back into a child. Quickly, she touched another, then another. Soon the castle was ringing with children's voices, and all of them were clamoring to escape.

But before they could move, the mermaid was there! She glared at the children, she glared at Meaghan, she glared at Ewan. Never had she looked more dangerous. Never had she looked more beautiful.

As the children stood frozen, the mermaid seemed to grow. She swelled till her head touched the ceiling, and the tip of her tail touched the floor. Her hair curled around the room like a serpent's coil, then it began to wind around the children like a net.

Arianne wanted to keep all the children, but most of all, she wanted to punish Meaghan. She stretched out a long, white arm and pulled her off the floor. Meaghan wanted to scream, but she knew she had only seconds left. As she struggled, she struck the mermaid's wrist with the blade of the knife. Arianne gave a long, deep moan and turned into a sea bass.

Then Meaghan, Ewan and the children ran from the palace and up to the shore. And there, waiting for them, stood Merlin, barking with the pleasure of seeing them alive.

That night, all of the children were safely restored to their families. The next day, Meaghan and Ewan went with Merlin to thank the sea witch and return her knife. From then on, when they walked in the evenings on the shore by the sea, they looked very hard at the sea bass. For both of them knew that one of those shimmering fishes had once been Arianne.

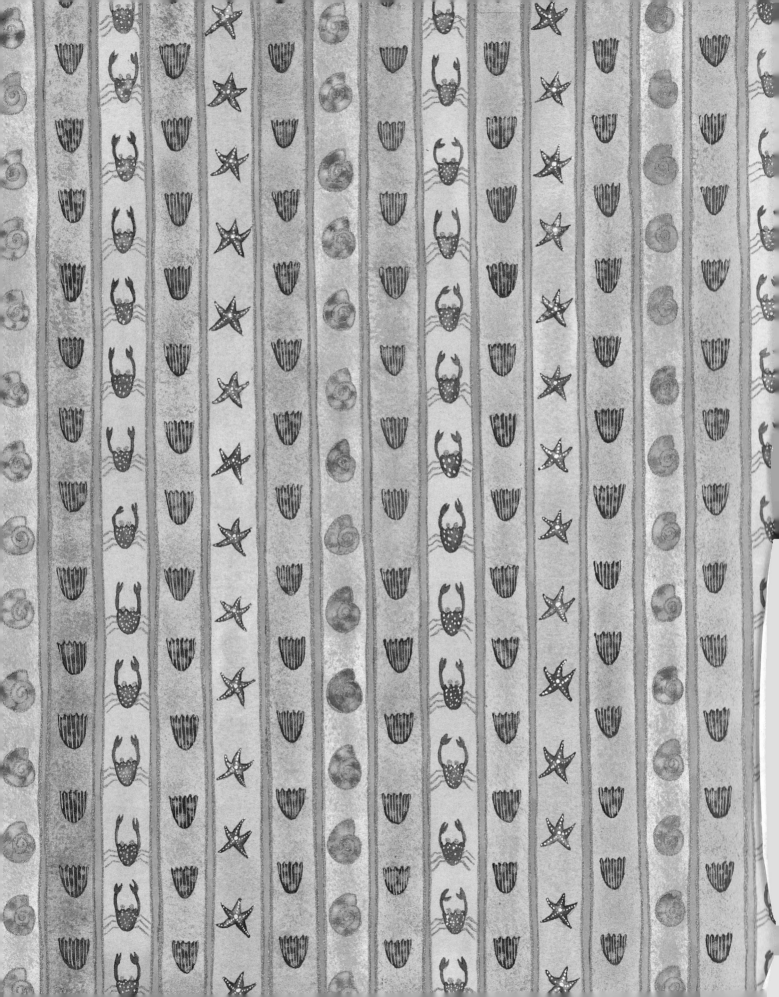

BAREFOOT BOOKS publishes high-quality picture books for children of all ages and specializes in the work of artists and writers from many cultures. If you have enjoyed this book and would like to receive a copy of our current catalog, please contact our New York office:

tel: 718 260 8946   fax: 1 888 346 9138 (toll free)

e-mail: ussales@barefoot.books.com

website: www.barefoot-books.com

Barefoot Books Inc.
41 Schermerhorn Street, Suite 145
Brooklyn, New York
NY 11201-4845

ISBN 1 902283 40 6

This book has been printed on 100% acid-free paper
Typeset in Goudy Infant 17 point on 22 point leading
The illustrations were prepared in watercolor and ink on 140gsm watercolor paper
Graphic design by Judy Linard, London
Color separation by Grafiscan, Verona
Printed and bound in Singapore by Tien Wah Press (Pte) Ltd

1 3 5 7 9 8 6 4 2